Robert Seymour Bridges

The Shorter Poems of Robert Bridges

Robert Seymour Bridges

The Shorter Poems of Robert Bridges

ISBN/EAN: 9783744770378

Printed in Europe, USA, Canada, Australia, Japan

Cover: Foto ©Andreas Hilbeck / pixelio.de

More available books at **www.hansebooks.com**

THE SHORTER

·POEMS

OF

ROBERT BRIDGES

THE SHORTER
POEMS

OF

ROBERT BRIDGES

GEO BELL & SONS LONDON

1896

BOOK I.

ERRATA.

p. 44, l. 16, *for* empty *read* airy
p. 80, l. 25, *for* trees *read* the trees

1.

ELEGY.

CLEAR and gentle stream!
Known and loved so long,
That hast heard the song,
And the idle dream
Of my boyish day;
While I once again
Down thy margin stray,
In the selfsame strain
Still my voice is spent,
With my old lament,
And my idle dream,
Clear and gentle stream!

Where my old seat was
Here again I sit,
Where the long boughs knit
Over stream and grass
A translucent eaves:
Where back eddies play
Shipwreck with the leaves,
And the proud swans stray,
Sailing one by one
Out of stream and sun,
And the fish lie cool
In their chosen pool.

Many an afternoon
Of the summer day
Dreaming here I lay;
And I know how soon,
Idly at its hour,
First the deep bell hums
From the minster tower,
And then evening comes,
Creeping up the glade,
With her lengthening shade,
And the tardy boon,
Of her brightening moon.

Clear and gentle stream!
Ere again I go
Where thou dost not flow,
Well does it beseem
Thee to hear again
Once my youthful song,
That familiar strain
Silent now so long:
Be as I content
With my old lament,
And my idle dream,
Clear and gentle stream!

II.

ELEGY.

THE wood is bare: a river-mist is steeping
　　The trees that winter's chill of life bereaves.
Only their stiffened boughs break silence, weeping
　　Over their fallen leaves:

That lie upon the dank earth brown and rotten,
  Miry and matted in the soaking wet:
Forgotten with the spring, that is forgotten
    By them that can forget.

Yet it was here we walked when ferns were springing,
  And through the mossy bank shot bud and blade:—
Here found in summer, when the birds were singing,
    A green and pleasant shade.

'Twas here we loved in sunnier days and greener;
  And now, in this disconsolate decay,
I come to see her where I most have seen her,
    And touch the happier day.

For on this path, at every turn and corner,
  The fancy of her figure on me falls:
Yet walks she with the slow step of a mourner,
    Nor hears my voice that calls.

So through my heart there winds a track of feeling,
  A path of memory, that is all her own:
Whereto her ghostly figure ever stealing
    Haunts the sad spot alone.

About her steps the trunks are bare, the branches
  Drip heavy tears upon her downcast head;
And bleed from unseen wounds no warm sun staunches,
    For the year's sun is dead.

And dead leaves wrap the fruits that summer planted:
  And birds that love the South have taken wing.
The wanderer, loitering o'er the scene enchanted,
    Weeps, and despairs of spring.

———

III.

Poor withered rose and dry,
  Skeleton of a rose,
Risen to testify
  To love's sad close:

Treasured for love's sweet sake
  That of joy past
Thou might'st again awake
  Memory at last.

Yet is thy perfume sweet;
  Thy petals red
Yet tell of summer heat,
  And the gay bed:

Yet yet recall the glow
  Of the gazing sun,
When at thy bush we two
  Joined hands in one.

But, rose, thou hast not seen,
  Thou hast not wept
The change that passed between,
  Whilst thou hast slept.

To me thou seemest yet
  The dead dream's thrall:
While I live and forget
  Dream, truth and all.

Thou art more fresh than I,
  Rose, sweet and red:
Salt on my pale cheeks lie
  The tears I shed.

IV.

THE cliff-top has a carpet
  Of lilac gold and green:
The blue sky bounds the ocean,
  The white clouds scud between.

A flock of gulls are wheeling
  And wailing round my seat;
Above my head the heaven,
  The sea beneath my feet.

THE OCEAN.

Were I a cloud I'd gather
  My skirts up in the air,
And fly I well know whither,
  And rest I well know where.

As pointed the star surely,
  The legend tells of old,
Where the wise kings might offer
  Myrrh, frankincense, and gold;

Above the house I'd hover
  Where dwells my love, and wait
Till haply I might spy her
  Throw back the garden-gate.

There in the summer evening
  I would bedeck the moon;
I would float down, and screen her
  From the sun's rays at noon;

And if her flowers should languish,
  Or wither in the drought,
Upon her tall white lilies
  I'd pour my heart's blood out:

So if she wore one only,
  And shook not out the rain,
Were I a cloud, O cloudlet,
  I had not lived in vain.

A CLOUD.

But were I thou, O ocean,
  I would not chafe and fret
As thou, because a limit
  To thy desires is set.

I would be blue, and gentle,
  Patient, and calm, and see
If my smiles might not tempt her,
  My love, to come to me.

I'd make my depths transparent,
  And still, that she should lean
O'er the boat's edge, to ponder
  The sights that swam between.

I would command strange creatures,
  Of bright hue and quick fin,
To stir the water near her,
  And tempt her bare arm in.

I'd teach her spend the summer
  With me: and I can tell,
That, were I thou, O ocean,
  My love should love me well.

But on the mad cloud scudded,
  The breeze it blew so stiff;
And the sad ocean bellowed,
  And pounded at the cliff.

V.

I HEARD a linnet courting
His lady in the spring;
His mates were idly sporting,
Nor stayed to hear him sing
His song of love.—
I fear my speech distorting
His tender love.

One phrase was all his pleading,
He spoke of love and home:
To her who gave him heeding
He sang his question, 'Come.'—
His gay sweet notes,
So sadly marred in the reading!
His tender notes!

And when he ceased, the hearer
Re-echoed the refrain,
And swiftly perching nearer,
'Come, come,' she sang again.—
Ah for their loves!
Would that my verse spake clearer,
Their tender loves!

Blest union of twin creatures
Unmarred by sense of doubt:
All summer's dry misfeatures
Such springtide trust bars out;
But of their loves
Fall short our wiser natures:
Their tender loves!

VI.

DEAR lady, when thou frownest,
　　And my true love despisest,
And all thy vows disownest
　　That sealed my venture wisest;
I think thy pride's displeasure
Neglects a matchless treasure
Exceeding price and measure.

But when again thou smilest,
　　And love for love returnest,
And fear with joy beguilest,
　　And takest truth in earnest;
Then, though I sheer adore thee,
The sum of my love for thee
Seems poor, scant, and unworthy.

VII.

I WILL not let thee go.
Ends all our month-long love in this?
　　Can it be summed up so,
　　Quit in a single kiss?
I will not let thee go.

I will not let thee go.
If thy words' breath could scare thy deeds,
　　As the soft south can blow
　　And toss the feathered seeds,
　　Then might I let thee go.

I will not let thee go.
Had not the great sun seen, I might;
　　Or were he reckoned slow
　　To bring the false to light,
　　Then might I let thee go.

I will not let thee go.
The stars that crowd the summer skies
 Have watched us so below
 With all their million eyes,
 I dare not let thee go.

I will not let thee go.
Have we not chid the changeful moon,
 Now rising late, and now
 Because she set too soon,
 And shall I let thee go?

I will not let thee go.
Have not the young flowers been content,
 Plucked ere their buds could blow,
 To seal our sacrament?
 I cannot let thee go.

I will not let thee go.
I hold thee by too many bands:
 Thou sayest farewell, and lo!
 I have thee by the hands,
 And will not let thee go.

VIII.

I FOUND to-day out walking
 The flower my love loves best.
What when I stooped to pluck it,
 Could dare my hand arrest?

Was it a snake lay curling
 About the root's thick crown?
Or did some hidden bramble
 Tear my hand reaching down?

There was no snake uncurling,
 And no thorn wounded me;

'Twas my heart checked me, sighing
She is beyond the sea.

IX.

A POPPY grows upon the shore,
Bursts her twin cup in summer late:
Her leaves are glaucous green and hoar,
Her petals yellow, delicate.

Oft to her cousins turns her thought,
In wonder if they care that she
Is fed with spray for dew, and caught
By every gale that sweeps the sea.

She has no lovers like the red,
That dances with the noble corn:
Her blossoms on the waves are shed,
Where she stands shivering and forlorn.

X.

SOMETIMES when my lady sits by me
    My rapture 's so great, that I tear
My mind from the thought that she 's nigh me,
    And strive to forget that she 's there.
    And sometimes when she is away
Her absence so sorely does try me,
    That I shut to my eyes, and assay
To think she is there sitting by me.

XI.

LONG are the hours the sun is above,
But when evening comes I go home to my love.

I'm away the daylight hours and more,
Yet she comes not down to open the door.

She does not meet me upon the stair,—
She sits in my chamber and waits for me there.

As I enter the room she does not move :
I always walk straight up to my love;

And she lets me take my wonted place
At her side, and gaze in her dear dear face.

There as I sit, from her head thrown back
Her hair falls straight in a shadow black.

Aching and hot as my tired eyes be,
She is all that I wish to see.

And in my wearied and toil-dinned ear,
She says all things that I wish to hear.

Dusky and duskier grows the room,
Yet I see her best in the darker gloom.

When the winter eves are early and cold,
The firelight hours are a dream of gold.

And so I sit here night by night,
In rest and enjoyment of love's delight.

But a knock at the door, a step on the stair
Will startle, alas, my love from her chair.

If a stranger comes she will not stay:
At the first alarm she is off and away.

And he wonders, my guest, usurping her throne,
That I sit so much by myself alone.

———

XII.

WHO has not walked upon the shore,
And who does not the morning know,
The day the angry gale is o'er,
The hour the wind has ceased to blow?

The horses of the strong south-west
Are pastured round his tropic tent,
Careless how long the ocean's breast
Sob on and sigh for passion spent.

The frightened birds, that fled inland
To house in rock and tower and tree,
Are gathering on the peaceful strand,
To tempt again the sunny sea;

Whereon the timid ships steal out
And laugh to find their foe asleep,
That lately scattered them about,
And drave them to the fold like sheep.

The snow-white clouds he northward chased
Break into phalanx, line, and band:
All one way to the south they haste,
The south, their pleasant fatherland.

From distant hills their shadows creep,
Arrive in turn and mount the lea,
And flit across the downs, and leap
Sheer off the cliff upon the sea;

And sail and sail far out of sight.
But still I watch their fleecy trains,
That piling all the south with light,
Dapple in France the fertile plains.

XIII.

I MADE another song,
In likeness of my love :
And sang it all day long,
Around, beneath, above ;
I told my secret out,
That none might be in doubt.

I sang it to the sky,
That veiled his face to hear
How far her azure eye
Outdoes his splendid sphere ;
But at her eyelids' name
His white clouds fled for shame.

I told it to the trees,
And to the flowers confest,
And said not one of these
Is like my lily drest ;
Nor spathe nor petal dared
Vie with her body bared.

I shouted to the sea,
That set his waves a-prance ;
Her floating hair is free,
Free are her feet to dance ;
And for thy wrath, I swear
Her frown is more to fear.

And as in happy mood
I walked and sang alone,
At eve beside the wood
I met my love, my own :
And sang to her the song
I had sung all day long.

XIV.

ELEGY

ON A LADY, WHOM GRIEF FOR THE DEATH OF HER
BETROTHED KILLED.

ASSEMBLE, all ye maidens, at the door,
And all ye loves, assemble; far and wide
Proclaim the bridal, that proclaimed before
Has been deferred to this late eventide:
    For on this night the bride,
      The days of her betrothal over,
   Leaves the parental hearth for evermore;
To-night the bride goes forth to meet her lover.

Reach down the wedding vesture, that has lain
   Yet all unvisited, the silken gown:
Bring out the bracelets, and the golden chain
   Her dearer friends provided: sere and brown
      Bring out the festal crown,
    And set it on her forehead lightly:
   Though it be withered, twine no wreath again;
This only is the crown she can wear rightly.

Cloke her in ermine, for the night is cold,
And wrap her warmly, for the night is long,
In pious hands the flaming torches hold,
While her attendants, chosen from among
      Her faithful virgin throng,
    May lay her in her cedar litter,
   Decking her coverlet with sprigs of gold,
Roses, and lilies white that best befit her.

Sound flute and tabor, that the bridal be
Not without music, nor with these alone;

But let the viol lead the melody,
With lesser intervals, and plaintive moan
    Of sinking semitone;
  And, all in choir, the virgin voices
 Rest not from singing in skilled harmony
The song that aye the bridegroom's ear rejoices.

Let the priests go before, arrayed in white,
And let the dark stoled minstrels follow slow,
Next they that bear her, honoured on this night,
And then the maidens, in a double row,
    Each singing soft and low,
  And each on high a torch upstaying:
Unto her lover lead her forth with light,
With music, and with singing, and with praying.

'Twas at this sheltering hour he nightly came,
And found her trusty window open wide,
And knew the signal of the timorous flame,
That long the restless curtain would not hide
    Her form that stood beside;
  As scarce she dared to be delighted,
 Listening to that sweet tale, that is no shame
To faithful lovers, that their hearts have plighted.

But now for many days the dewy grass
Has shown no markings of his feet at morn:
And watching she has seen no shadow pass
The moonlit walk, and heard no music borne
    Upon her ear forlorn.
  In vain has she looked out to greet him;
He has not come, he will not come, alas!
So let us bear her out where she must meet him.

  Now to the river bank the priests are come:
The bark is ready to receive its freight:
            c

Let some prepare her place therein, and some
Embark the litter with its slender weight:
    The rest stand by in state,
  And sing her a safe passage over;
  While she is oared across to her new home,
Into the arms of her expectant lover.

And thou, O lover, that art on the watch,
Where, on the banks of the forgetful streams,
The pale indifferent ghosts wander, and snatch
The sweeter moments of their broken dreams,—
    Thou, when the torchlight gleams,
  When thou shalt see the slow procession,
  And when thine ears the fitful music catch,
Rejoice! for thou art near to thy possession.

XV.

RONDEAU.

His poisoned shafts, that fresh he dips
In juice of plants that no bee sips,
  He takes, and with his bow renown'd
  Goes out upon his hunting ground,
Hanging his quiver at his hips.

He draws them one by one, and clips
Their heads between his finger-tips,
  And looses with a twanging sound
      His poisoned shafts.

But if a maiden with her lips
Suck from the wound the blood that drips,
  And drink the poison from the wound,
  The simple remedy is found
That of their deadly terror strips
      His poisoned shafts.

XVI.

TRIOLET.

WHEN first we met we did not guess
That Love would prove so hard a master;
Of more than common friendliness
When first we met we did not guess.
Who could foretell this sore distress,
This irretrievable disaster
When first we met?—We did not guess
That Love would prove so hard a master.

XVII.

TRIOLET.

ALL women born are so perverse
No man need boast their love possessing.
If nought seem better, nothing's worse:
All women born are so perverse.
From Adam's wife, that proved a curse
Though God had made her for a blessing,
All women born are so perverse
No man need boast their love possessing.

BOOK II.

I.

MUSE.

WILL Love again awake,
That lies asleep so long?

POET.

O hush! ye tongues that shake
The drowsy night with song.

MUSE.

It is a lady fair
Whom once he deigned to praise,
That at the door doth dare
Her sad complaint to raise.

POET.

She must be fair of face,
As bold of heart she seems,
If she would match her grace
With the delight of dreams.

MUSE.

Her beauty would surprise
Gazers on Autumn eves,
Who watched the broad moon rise
Upon the scattered sheaves.

POET.

O sweet must be the voice
He shall descend to hear,
Who doth in Heaven rejoice
His most enchanted ear.

MUSE.

The smile, that rests to play
Upon her lip, foretells
What musical array
Tricks her sweet syllables.

POET.

And yet her smiles have danced
In vain, if her discourse
Win not the soul entranced
In divine intercourse.

MUSE.

She will encounter all
This trial without shame,
Her eyes men Beauty call,
And Wisdom is her name.

POET.

Throw back the portals then,
Ye guards, your watch that keep,
Love will awake again
That lay so long asleep.

II.

A PASSER BY.

WHITHER, O splendid ship, thy white sails crowding,
　Leaning across the bosom of the urgent West,
That fearest nor sea rising, nor sky clouding,
　Whither away, fair rover, and what thy quest?

Ah! soon, when Winter has all our vales opprest,
When skies are cold and misty, and hail is hurling,
　Wilt thóu glíde on the blue Pacific, or rest
In a summer haven asleep, thy white sails furling.

I there before thee, in the country so well thou
　　knowest,
　Already arrived am inhaling the odorous air :
I watch thee enter unerringly where thou goest,
　And anchor queen of the strange shipping there,
　Thy sails for awnings spread, thy masts bare:
Nor is aught from the foaming reef to the snow-
　　capped, grandest
Peak, that is over the feathery palms more fair
Than thou, so upright, so stately, and still thou
　　standest.

And yet, O splendid ship, unhailed and nameless,
　I know not if, aiming a fancy, I rightly divine
That thou hast a purpose joyful, a courage blameless,
　Thy port assured in a happier land than mine.
　But for all I have given thee, beauty enough is
　　thine,
　As thou, aslant with trim tackle and shrouding,
　From the proud nostril curve of a prow's line
In the offing scatterest foam, thy white sails crowding.

III.

LATE SPRING EVENING.

I saw the Virgin-mother clad in green,
Walking the sprinkled meadows at sundown;
While yet the moon's cold flame was hung between
The day and night, above the dusky town:

I saw her brighter than the Western gold,
Whereto she faced in splendour to behold.

Her dress was greener than the tenderest leaf
That trembled in the sunset glare aglow:
Herself more delicate than is the brief,
Pink apple-blossom, that May showers lay low,
And more delicious than 's the earliest streak
The blushing rose shows of her crimson cheek.

As if to match the sight that so did please,
A music entered, making passion fain:
Three nightingales sat singing in the trees,
And praised the Goddess for the fallen rain;
Which yet their unseen motions did arouse,
Or parting Zephyrs shook out from the boughs.

And o'er the treetops, scattered in mid air,
The exhausted clouds, laden with crimson light
Floated, or seemed to sleep; and, highest there,
One planet broke the lingering ranks of night;
Daring day's company, so he might spy
The Virgin-queen once with his watchful eye.

And when I saw her, then I worshipped her,
And said,—O bounteous Spring, O beauteous Spring,
Mother of all my years, thou who dost stir
My heart to adore thee and my tongue to sing,
Flower of my fruit, of my heart's blood the fire,
Of all my satisfaction the desire!

How art thou every year more beautiful,
Younger for all the winters thou hast cast:
And I, for all my love grows, grow more dull,
Decaying with each season overpast!
In vain to teach him love must man employ thee,
The more he learns the less he can enjoy thee.

IV.

WOOING.

I KNOW not how I came,
New on my knightly journey,
 To win the fairest dame
That graced my maiden tourney.

Chivalry's lovely prize
With all men's gaze upon her,
 Why did she free her eyes
On me, to do me honour?

Ah! ne'er had I my mind
With such high hope delighted,
 Had she not first inclined,
And with her eyes invited.

But never doubt I knew,
Having their glance to cheer me,
 Until the day joy grew
Too great, too sure, too near me.

When hope a fear became,
And passion, grown too tender,
 Now trembled at the shame
Of a despised surrender;

And where my love at first
Saw kindness in her smiling,
 I read her pride, and cursed
The arts of her beguiling.

Till winning less than won,
And liker wooed than wooing,
 Too late I turned undone
Away from my undoing;

And stood beside the door,
Whereto she followed, making
My hard leave-taking more
Hard by her sweet leave-taking.

Her speech would have betrayed
Her thought, had mine been colder:
Her eyes distress had made
A lesser lover bolder.

But no! Fond heart, distrust,
Cried Wisdom, and consider:
Go free, since go thou must,
And so farewell I bid her.

And brisk upon my way
I smote the stroke to sever,
And should have lost that day
My life's delight for ever;

But when I saw her start
And turn aside and tremble;—
Ah! she was true, her heart
I knew did not dissemble.

V.

THERE is a hill beside the silver Thames,
Shady with birch and beech and odorous pine:
And brilliant underfoot with thousand gems
Steeply the thickets to his floods decline.
Straight trees in every place
Their thick tops interlace,
And pendant branches trail their foliage fine
Upon his watery face.

Swift from the sweltering pasturage he flows :
His stream, alert to seek the pleasant shade,
Pictures his gentle purpose, as he goes
Straight to the caverned pool his toil has made.
    His winter floods lay bare
    The stout roots in the air :
His summer streams are cool, when they have played
    Among their fibrous hair.

A rushy island guards the sacred bower,
And hides it from the meadow, where in peace
The lazy cows wrench many a scented flower,
Robbing the golden market of the bees :
    And laden barges float
    By banks of myosote ;
And scented flag and golden flower-de-lys
    Delay the loitering boat.

And on this side the island, where the pool
Eddies away, are tangled mass on mass
The water-weeds, that net the fishes cool,
And scarce allow a narrow stream to pass;
    Where spreading crowfoot mars
    The drowning nenuphars,
Waving the tassels of her silken grass
    Below her silver stars.

But in the purple pool there nothing grows,
Not the white water-lily spoked with gold ;
Though best she loves the hollows, and well knows
On quiet streams her broad shields to unfold :
    Yet should her roots but try
    Within these deeps to lie,
Not her long reaching stalk could ever hold
    Her waxen head so high.

Sometimes an angler comes, and drops his hook
Within its hidden depths, and 'gainst a tree
Leaning his rod, reads in some pleasant book,
Forgetting soon his pride of fishery;
  And dreams, or falls asleep,
  While curious fishes peep
About his nibbled bait, or scornfully
  Dart off and rise and leap.

And sometimes a slow figure 'neath the trees,
In ancient-fashioned smock, with tottering care,
Upon a staff propping his weary knees,
May by the pathway of the forest fare:
  ·As from a buried day
  Across the mind will stray
Some perishing mute shadow,—and unaware
  He passeth on his way.

Else, he that wishes solitude is safe,
Whether he bathe at morning in the stream:
Or lead his love there when the hot hours chafe
The meadows, busy with a blurring steam;
  Or watch, as fades the light,
  The gibbous moon grow bright,
Until her magic rays dance in a dream,
  And glorify the night.

Where is this bower beside the silver Thames?
O pool and flowery thickets, hear my vow!
O trees of freshest foliage and straight stems,
No sharer of my secret I allow:
  Lest ere I come the while
  Strange feet your shades defile;
Or lest the burly oarsman turn his prow
  Within your guardian isle.

VI.

A WATER-PARTY.

LET us, as by this verdant bank we float,
Search down the marge to find some shady pool;
Where we may rest awhile and moor our boat,
And bathe our tired limbs in the waters cool.
        Beneath the noonday sun,
        Swiftly, O river, run!

Here is a mirror for Narcissus, see!
I cannot sound it, plumbing with my oar.
Lay the stern in beneath this bowering tree!
Now, stepping on this stump, we are ashore.
        Guard, Hamadryades,
        Our clothes laid by your trees!

How the birds warble in the woods! I pick
The waxen lilies, diving to the root.
But swim not far in the stream, the weeds grow
    thick,
And hot on the bare head the sunbeams shoot.
        Until our sport be done,
        O merry birds sing on!

If but to-night the sky be clear, the moon
Will serve us well, for she is near the full.
We shall row safely home; only too soon,—
So pleasant 'tis, whether we float or pull.
        To guide us through the night,
        O summer moon, shine bright!

VII.

THE DOWNS.

O BOLD majestic downs, smooth, fair and lonely;
O still solitude, only matched in the skies :
    Perilous in steep places,
    Soft in the level races,
Where sweeping in phantom silence the cloudland flies ;
With lovely undulation of fall and rise ;
    Entrenched with thickets thorned,
By delicate miniature dainty flowers adorned !

I climb your crown, and lo ! a sight surprising
Of sea in front uprising, steep and wide :
    And scattered ships ascending
    To heaven, lost in the blending
Of distant blues, where water and sky divide,
Urging their engines against wind and tide,
    And all so small and slow
They seem to be wearily pointing the way they would
    go.

The accumulated murmur of soft plashing,
Of waves on rocks dashing, and searching the sands
    Takes my ear, in the veering
    Baffled wind, as rearing
Upright at the cliff, to the gullies and rifts he stands ;
And his conquering surges scour out over the lands;
    While again at the foot of the downs
He masses his strength to recover the topmost crowns.

———

VIII.

SPRING.

ODE I.

INVITATION TO THE COUNTRY.

AGAIN with pleasant green
Has Spring renewed the wood,
And where the bare trunks stood
Are leafy arbours seen;
And back on budding boughs
Come birds, to court and pair,
Whose rival amorous vows
Amaze the scented air.

The freshets are unbound,
And leaping from the hill,
Their mossy banks refill
With streams of light and sound:
And scattered down the meads,
From hour to hour unfold
A thousand buds and beads
In stars and cups of gold.

Now hear, and see, and note,
The farms are all astir,
And every labourer
Has doffed his winter coat;
And how with specks of white
They dot the brown hillside,
Or jaunt and sing outright
As by their teams they stride.

D

They sing to feel the Sun
Regain his wanton strength;
To know the year at length
Rewards their labour done;
To see the rootless stake
They set bare in the ground,
Burst into leaf, and shake
Its grateful scent around.

Ah now an evil lot
Is his, who toils for gain,
Where crowded chimneys stain
The heavens his choice forgot;
'Tis on the blighted trees
That deck his garden dim,
And in the tainted breeze,
That sweet spring comes to him.

Far sooner I would choose
The life of brutes that bask,
Than set myself a task,
Which inborn powers refuse:
And rather far enjoy
The body, than invent
A duty, to destroy
The ease which nature sent;

And country life I praise,
And lead, because I find
The philosophic mind
Can take no middle ways;
She will not leave her love
To mix with men, her art
Is all to strive above
The crowd, or stand apart.

Thrice happy he, the rare
Prometheus, who can play
With hidden things, and lay
New realms of nature bare;
Whose venturous step has trod
Hell underfoot, and won
A crown from man and God
For all that he has done.—

That highest gift of all,
Since crabbèd fate did flood
My heart with sluggish blood, '
I look not mine to call;
But, like a truant freed,
Fly to the woods, and claim
A pleasure for the deed
Of my inglorious name:

And am content, denied
The best, in choosing right;
For Nature can delight
Fancies unoccupied
With ecstasies so sweet
As none can even guess,
Who walk not with the feet
Of joy in idleness.

Then leave your joyless ways,
My friend, my joys to see.
The day you come shall be
The choice of chosen days:
You shall be lost, and learn
New being, and forget
The world, till your return
Shall bring your first regret.

IX.

SPRING.

ODE II.

REPLY.

BEHOLD! the radiant Spring,
In splendour decked anew,
Down from her heaven of blue
Returns on sunlit wing:
The zephyrs of her train
In fleecy clouds disport,
And birds to greet her reign
Summon their silvan court.

And here in street and square
The prisoned trees contest
Her favour with the best,
To robe themselves full fair:
And forth their buds provoke,
Forgetting winter brown,
And all the mire and smoke
That wrapped the dingy town.

Now he that loves indeed
His pleasure must awake,
Lest any pleasure take
Its flight, and he not heed;
For of his few short years
Another now invites
His hungry soul, and cheers
His life with new delights.

And who loves Nature more
Than he, whose painful art
Has taught and skilled his heart
To read her skill and lore?
Whose spirit leaps more high,
Plucking the pale primrose,
Than his whose feet must fly
The pasture where it grows?

One long in city pent
Forgets, or must complain:
But think not I can stain
My heaven with discontent;
Nor wallow with that sad,
Backsliding herd, who cry
That Truth must make man bad,
And pleasure is a lie.

Rather while Reason lives
To mark me from the beast,
I'll teach her serve at least
To heal the wound she gives:
Nor need she strain her powers
Beyond a common flight,
To make the passing hours
Happy from morn till night.

Since health our toil rewards,
And strength is labour's prize,
I hate not, nor despise
The work my lot accords;
Nor fret with fears unkind
The tender joys, that bless
My hard-won peace of mind,
In hours of idleness.

Then what charm company
Can give, know I,—if wine
Go round, or throats combine
To set dumb music free.
Or deep in wintertide
When winds without make moan,
I love my own fireside
Not least when most alone.

Then oft I turn the page
In which our country's name,
Spoiling the Greek of fame,
Shall sound in every age:
Or some Terentian play
Renew, whose excellent
Adjusted folds betray
How once Menander went.

Or if grave study suit
The yet unwearied brain,
Plato can teach again,
And Socrates dispute;
Till fancy in a dream
Confront their souls with mine,
Crowning the mind supreme,
And her delights divine.

While pleasure yet can be
Pleasant, and fancy sweet,
I bid all care retreat,
From my philosophy;
Which, when I come to try
Your simpler life, will find,
I doubt not, joys to vie
With those I leave behind.

X.

ELEGY.

AMONG THE TOMBS.

SAD, sombre place, beneath whose antique yews
I come, unquiet sorrows to control;
Amid thy silent mossgrown graves to muse
With my neglected solitary soul;
And to poetic sadness care confide,
Trusting sweet Melancholy for my guide:

They will not ask why in thy shades I stray,
Among the tombs finding my rare delight,
Beneath the sun at indolent noonday,
Or in the windy moon-enchanted night,
Who have once reined in their steeds at any shrine,
And given them water from the well divine.—

The orchards are all ripened, and the sun
Spots the deserted gleanings with decay;
The seeds are perfected: his work is done,
And Autumn lingers but to outsmile the May;
Bidding his tinted leaves glide, bidding clear
Unto clear skies the birds applaud the year.

Lo, here I sit, and to the world I call,
The world my solemn fancy leaves behind,
Come! pass within the inviolable wall,
Come pride, come pleasure, come distracted mind;
Within the fated refuge, hither, turn,
And learn your wisdom ere 'tis late to learn.

Come with me now, and taste the fount of tears;
For many eyes have sanctified this spot,
Where grief's unbroken lineage endears
The charm untimely Folly injures not,

And slays the intruding thoughts, that overleap
The simple fence its holiness doth keep.

Read the worn names of the forgotten dead,
Their pompous legends will no smile awake;
Even the vainglorious title o'er the head
Wins its pride pardon for its sorrow's sake;
And carven Loves scorn not their dusty prize,
Though fallen so far from tender sympathies.

Here where a mother laid her only son,
Here where a lover left his bride, below
The treasured names their own are added on
To those whom they have followed long ago:
Sealing the record of the tears they shed,
That 'where their treasure there their hearts are fled.'

Grandfather, father, son, and then again
Child, grandchild, and great grandchild laid beneath,
Numbered in turn among the sons of men,
And gathered each one in his turn to death:
While he that occupies their house and name
To-day,—to-morrow too their grave shall claim.

And where are all their spirits? Ah! could we tell
The manner of our being when we die,
And see beyond the scene we know so well
The country that so much obscured doth lie!
With brightest visions our fond hopes repair,
Or crown our melancholy with despair;

From death, still death, still would a comfort come:
Since of this world the essential joy must fall
In all distributed, in each thing some,
In nothing all, and all complete in all;
Till pleasure, ageing to her full increase,
Puts on perfection, and is throned in peace.

Yea, sweetest peace, unsought-for, undesired,
Loathed and misnamed, 'tis thee I worship here :
Though in most black habiliments attired,
Thou art sweet peace, and thee I cannot fear.
Nay, were my last hope quenched, I here would sit
And praise the annihilation of the pit.

Nor quickly disenchanted will my feet
Back to the busy town return, but yet
Linger, ere I my loving friends would greet,
Or touch their hands, or share without regret
The warmth of that kind hearth, whose sacred ties
Only shall dim 'with tears my dying eyes.

XI.

DEJECTION.

WHEREFORE to-night so full of care,
My soul, revolving hopeless strife,
Pointing at hindrance, and the bare
Painful escapes of fitful life ?

Shaping the doom that may befall
By precedent of terror past :
By love dishonoured, and the call
Of friendship slighted at the last ?

By treasured names, the little store
That memory out of wreck could save
Of loving hearts, that gone before
Call their old comrade to the grave ?

O soul be patient: thou shalt find
A little matter mend all this;
Some strain of music to thy mind,
Some praise for skill not spent amiss.

Again shall pleasure overflow
Thy cup with sweetness, thou shalt taste
Nothing but sweetness, and shalt grow
Half sad for sweetness run to waste.

O happy life! I hear thee sing,
O rare delight of mortal stuff!
I praise my days for all they bring,
Yet are they only not enough.

XII.

MORNING HYMN.

O GOLDEN Sun, whose ray
My path illumineth:
Light of the circling day,
Whose night is birth and death:

That dost not stint the prime
Of wise and strong, nor stay
The changeful ordering time,
That brings their sure decay.

Though thou, the central sphere,
Dost seem to turn around
Thy creature world, and near
As father fond art found;

Thereon, as from above
To shine, and make rejoice
With beauty, life, and love,
The garden of thy choice.

To dress the jocund Spring
With bounteous promise gay
Of hotter months, that bring
The full perfected day;

To touch with richest gold
The ripe fruit, ere it fall;
And smile through cloud and cold
On Winter's funeral.

Now with resplendent flood
Gladden my waking eyes,
And stir my slothful blood
To joyous enterprise.

Arise, arise, as when
At first God said LIGHT BE!
That He might make us men
With eyes His light to see.

Scatter the clouds that hide
The face of heaven, and show
Where sweet Peace doth abide,
Where Truth and Beauty grow.

Awaken, cheer, adorn,
Invite, inspire, assure
The joys that praise thy morn,
The toil thy noons mature:

And soothe the eve of day,
That darkens back to death;
O golden Sun, whose ray
Our path illumineth!

XIII.

I HAVE loved flowers that fade,
Within whose magic tents
Rich hues have marriage made
With sweet unmemoried scents:

A honeymoon delight,—
A joy of love at sight,
That ages in an hour:—
My song be like a flower!

I have loved airs, that die
Before their charm is writ
Along a liquid sky
Trembling to welcome it.
Notes, that with pulse of fire
Proclaim the spirit's desire,
Then die, and are nowhere:—
My song be like an air!

Die, song, die like a breath,
And wither as a bloom:
Fear not a flowery death,
Dread not an empty tomb!
Fly with delight, fly hence!
'Twas thine love's tender sense
To feast, now on thy bier
Beauty shall shed a tear.

BOOK III.

I.

O MY vague desires!
Ye lambent flames of the soul, her offspring fires:
That are my soul herself in pangs sublime
Rising and flying to heaven before her time:

What doth tempt you forth
To drown in the south or shiver in the frosty north?
What seek ye or find ye in your random flying,
Ever soaring aloft, soaring and dying?

Joy, the joy of flight!
They hide in the sun, they flare and dance in the
    night;
Gone up, gone out of sight: and ever again
Follow fresh tongues of fire, fresh pangs of pain.

Ah! they burn my soul,
The fires, devour my soul that once was whole:
She is scattered in fiery phantoms day by day,
But whither, whither? ay whither? away, away?

Could I but control!
These vague desires, these leaping flames of the soul:
Could I but quench the fire! ah! could I stay
My soul that flieth, alas, and dieth away!

———

II.

LONDON SNOW.

WHEN men were all asleep the snow came flying,
In large white flakes falling on the city brown,
Stealthily and perpetually settling and loosely lying,
    Hushing the latest traffic of the drowsy town;
Deadening, muffling, stifling its murmurs failing;
Lazily and incessantly floating down and down:
    Silently sifting and veiling road, roof and railing;
Hiding difference, making unevenness even,
Into angles and crevices softly drifting and sailing.
    All night it fell, and when full inches seven
It lay in the depth of its uncompacted lightness,
Its clouds blew off from a high and frosty heaven;
    And all woke earlier for the unaccustomed brightness
Of the winter dawning, the strange unheavenly glare:
The eye marvelled—marvelled at the dazzling whiteness;
    The ear hearkened to the stillness of the solemn air;
No sound of wheel rumbling nor of foot falling,
And the busy morning cries came thin and spare.
    Then boys I heard, as they went to school, calling,
They gathered up the crystal manna to freeze
Their tongues with tasting, their hands with snow-
        balling;
    Or rioted in a drift, plunging up to the knees;
Or peering up from under the white-mossed wonder,
'O look at the trees!' they cried, 'O look at the trees!'
    With lessened load a few carts creak and blunder,
Following along the white deserted way,
A country company long dispersed asunder:
    When now already the sun, in pale display

Standing by Paul's high dome, spread forth below
His sparkling beams, and awoke the stir of thé day.
  For now doors open, and war is waged with the
      snow;
And trains of sombre men, past tale of number,
Tread long brown paths, as toward their toil they go:
  But even for them awhile no cares encumber
Their minds diverted; the daily word unspoken,
The daily thoughts of labour and sorrow slumber
  At the sight of the beauty that greets them, for the
      charm they have broken.

III.

THE VOICE OF NATURE.

I STAND on the cliff and watch the veiled sun paling
  A silver field afar in the mournful sea,
The scourge of the surf, and plaintive gulls sailing
  At ease on the gale that smites the shuddering lea:
      Whose smile severe and chaste
June never hath stirred to vanity, nor age defaced.
In lofty thought strive, O spirit, for ever:
In courage and strength pursue thine own endeavour.

Ah! if it were only for thee, thou restless ocean
  Of waves that follow and roar, the sweep of the
      tides;
Wer't only for thee, impetuous wind, whose motion
  Precipitate all o'errides, and turns, nor abides:
      For you sad birds and fair,
  Or only for thee, bleak cliff, erect in the air;
Then well could I read wisdom in every feature,
O well should I understand the voice of Nature.

E

But far away, I think, in the Thames valley,
  The silent river glides by flowery banks:
And birds sing sweetly in branches that arch an alley
  Of cloistered trees, moss-grown in their ancient
    ranks:
      Where if a light air stray,
  'Tis laden with hum of bees and scent of may.
Love and peace be thine, O spirit, for ever:
Serve thy sweet desire: despise endeavour.

And if it were only for thee, entrancèd river,
  That scarce dost rock the lily on her airy stem,
Or stir a wave to murmur, or a rush to quiver;
  Wer't but for the woods, and summer asleep in
    them:
      For you my bowers green,
  My hedges of rose and woodbine, with walks be-
    tween,
Then well could I read wisdom in every feature,
O well should I understand the voice of Nature.

IV.

ON A DEAD CHILD.

PERFECT little body, without fault or stain on thee,
  With promise of strength and manhood full and fair!
    Though cold and stark and bare,
The bloom and the charm of life doth awhile remain
    on thee.

Thy mother's treasure wert thou;—alas! no longer
  To visit her heart with wondrous joy; to be
    Thy father's pride;—ah, he
Must gather his faith together, and his strength make
    stronger.

To me, as I move thee now in the last duty,
  Dost thou with a turn or gesture anon respond;
    Startling my fancy fond
With a chance attitude of the head, a freak of beauty.

Thy hand clasps, as 'twas wont, my finger, and holds it:
  But the grasp is the clasp of Death, heartbreaking
    and stiff;
    Yet feels to my hand as if
Twas still thy 'will, thy pleasure and trust that
    enfolds it.

So I lay thee there, thy sunken eyelids closing,—
  Go lie thou there in thy coffin, thy last little bed!—
    Propping thy wise, sad head,
Thy firm, pale hands across thy chest disposing.

So quiet! doth the change content thee?—Death,
    whither hath he taken thee?
  To a world, do I think, that rights the disaster of
    this?
    The vision of which I miss,
Who weep for the body, and wish but to warm thee
    and awaken thee?

Ah! little at best can all our hopes avail us
  To lift this sorrow, or cheer us, when in the dark,
    Unwilling, alone we embark,
And the things we have seen and have known and
    have heard of, fail us.

——— .

V.

THE PHILOSOPHER TO HIS MISTRESS.

BECAUSE thou canst not see,
Because thou canst not know
The black and hopeless woe
That hath encompassed me:
Because, should I confess
The thought of my despair,
My words would wound thee less
Than swords can hurt the air:

Because with thee I seem
As one invited near
To taste the faery cheer
Of spirits in a dream;
Of whom he knoweth nought
Save that they vie to make
All motion, voice and thought
A pleasure for his sake:

Therefore more sweet and strange
Has been the mystery
Of thy long love to me,
That doth not quit, nor change,
Nor tax my solemn heart,
That kisseth in a gloom,
Knowing not who thou art
That givest, nor to whom.

Therefore the tender touch
Is more; more dear the smile:
And thy light words beguile
My wisdom overmuch:

And O with swiftness fly
The fancies of my song
To happy worlds, where I
Still in thy love belong.

VI.

SONG.

HASTE on, my joys! your treasure lies
In swift, unceasing flight.
O haste : for while your beauty flies
I seize your full delight.
Lo! I have seen the scented flower,
Whose tender stems I cull,
For her brief date and meted hour
Appear more beautiful.

O youth, O strength, O most divine
For that so short ye prove;
Were but your rare gifts longer mine,
Ye scarce would win my love.
Nay, life itself the heart would spurn,
Did once the days restore
The days, that once enjoyed return,
Return—ah! nevermore.

VII.

INDOLENCE.

WE left the city when the summer day
Had verged already on its hot decline,
And charmèd Indolence in languor lay
In her gay gardens, 'neath her towers divine:
' Farewell,' we said, ' dear city of youth and dream!'
And in our boat we stepped and took the stream.

All through that idle afternoon we strayed
Upon our proposed travel well begun,
As loitering by the woodland's dreamy shade,
Past shallow islets floating in the sun,
Or searching down the banks for rarer flowers
We lingered out the pleasurable hours.

Till when that loveliest came, which mowers home
Turns from their longest labour, as we steered
Along a straitened channel flecked with foam,
We lost our landscape wide, and slowly neared
An ancient bridge, that like a blind wall lay
Low on its buried vaults to block the way.

Then soon the narrow tunnels broader showed,
Where with its arches three it sucked the mass
Of water, that in swirl thereunder flowed,
Or stood piled at the piers waiting to pass;
And pulling for the middle span, we drew
The tender blades aboard and floated through.

But past the bridge what change we found below!
The stream, that all day long had laughed and played
Betwixt the happy shires, ran dark and slow,
And with its easy flood no murmur made:
And weeds spread on its surface, and about
The stagnant margin reared their stout heads out.

Upon the left high elms, with giant wood
Skirting the water-meadows, interwove
Their slumbrous crowns, o'ershadowing where they
    stood
The floor and heavy pillars of the grove:
And in the shade, through reeds and sedges dank,
A footpath led along the moated bank.

Across, all down the right, an old brick wall,
Above and o'er the channel, red did lean;
Here buttressed up, and bulging there to fall,
Tufted with grass and plants and lichen green;
And crumbling to the flood, which at its base
Slid gently nor disturbed its mirrored face.

Sheer on the wall the houses rose, their backs
All windowless, neglected and awry,
With tottering coins, and crooked chimney stacks;
And here and there an unused door, set high
Above the fragments of its mouldering stair,
With rail and broken step led out on air.

Beyond, deserted wharfs and vacant sheds,
With empty boats and barges moored along,
And rafts half sunken, fringed with weedy shreds,
And sodden beams, once soaked to season strong.
No sight of man, nor sight of life, no stroke,
No voice the somnolence and silence broke.

Then I who rowed leant on my oar, whose drip
Fell without sparkle, and I rowed no more ;
And he that steered moved neither hand nor lip,
But turned his wondering eye from shore to shore;
And our trim boat let her swift motion die,
Between the dim reflections floating by.

VIII.

I PRAISE the tender flower,
   That on a mournful day
   Bloomed in my garden bower '
   And made the winter gay.
   Its loveliness contented
      My heart tormented.

I praise the gentle maid
Whose happy voice and smile
To confidence betrayed
My doleful heart awhile:
And gave my spirit deploring
    Fresh wings for soaring.

The maid for very fear
Of love I durst not tell:
The rose could never hear,
Though I bespake her well:
So in my song I bind them
    For all to find them.

IX.

A WINTER'S night with the snow about:
'Twas silent within and cold without:
Both father and mother to bed were gone:
The son sat yet by the fire alone.

He gazed on the fire, and dreamed again
Of one that was now no more among men:
As still he sat and never aware
How close was the spirit beside his chair.

Nay, sad were his thoughts, for he wept and said
Ah, woe for the dead! ah, woe for the dead!
How heavy the earth lies now on her breast,
The lips that I kissed, and the hand I pressed.

The spirit he saw not, he could not hear
The comforting words she spake in his ear:
His heart in the grave with her mouldering clay
No welcome gave—and she fled away.

X.

My bed and pillow are cold,
My heart is faint with dread,
The air hath an odour of mould,
I dream I lie with the dead:
  I cannot move,
  O come to me, love,
  Or else I am dead.

The feet I hear on the floor
Tread heavily overhead:
O Love, come down to the door,
Come, Love, come, ere I be dead:
  Make shine thy light,
  O Love, in the night;
  Or else I am dead.

XI.

O THOU unfaithful, still as ever dearest,
That in thy beauty to my eyes appearest,
In fancy rising now to re-awaken
  My love unshaken ;

All thou'st forgotten, but no change can free thee,
No hate unmake thee; as thou wert I see thee,
And am contented, eye from fond eye meeting
  Its ample greeting.

O thou my star of stars, among things wholly
Devoted, sacred, dim and melancholy,
The only joy of all the joys I cherished
  That hast not perished,

Why now on others squand'rest thou the treasure,
That to be jealous of is still my pleasure:

As still I dream 'tis me whom thou invitest,
    Me thou delightest ?

But day by day my joy hath feebler being,
The fading picture tires my painful seeing,
And faery fancy leaves her habitation
    To desolation.

Of two things open left for lovers parted
'Twas thine to scorn the past and go lighthearted:
But I would ever dream I still possess it,
    And thus caress it.

XII.

    THOU didst delight my eyes:
    Yet who am I? nor first
    Nor last nor best, that durst
    Once dream of thee for prize;
    Nor this the only time
    Thou shalt set love to rhyme.

    Thou didst delight my ear:
    Ah! little praise; thy voice
    Makes other hearts rejoice,
    Makes all ears glad that hear;
    And short my joy: but yet,
    O song, do not forget.

    For what wert thou to me?
    How shall I say? The moon,
    That poured her midnight noon
    Upon his wrecking sea;—
    A sail, that for a day
    Has cheered the castaway.

XIII.

Joy, sweetest lifeborn joy, where dost thou dwell?
Upon the formless moments of our being
Flitting, to mock the ear that heareth well,
To escape the trainèd eye that strains in seeing,
Dost thou fly with us whither we are fleeing;
Or home in our creations, to withstand
Blackwingèd death, that slays the making hand?

The making mind, that must untimely perish
Amidst its work which time may not destroy,
The beauteous forms which man shall love to cherish,
The glorious songs that combat earth's annoy?
Thou dost dwell here, I know, divinest Joy:
But they who build thy towers fair and strong,
Of all that toil, feel most of care and wrong.

Sense is so tender, O and hope so high,
That common pleasures mock their hope and sense;
And swifter than doth lightning from the sky
The ecstasy they pine for flashes hence,
Leaving the darkness and the woe immense,
Wherewith it seems no thread of life was woven,
Nor doth the track remain where once 'twas cloven.

And heaven and all the stable elements
That guard God's purpose mock us, though the mind
Be spent in searching: for his old intents
We see were never for our joy designed:
They shine as doth the bright sun on the blind,
Or like his pensioned stars, that hymn above
His praise, but not toward us, that God is Love.

For who so well hath wooed the maiden hours
As quite to have won the worth of their rich show,

To rob the night of mystery, or the flowers
Of their sweet delicacy ere they go?
Nay, even the dear occasion when we know,
We miss the joy, and on the gliding day
The special glories float and pass away.

Only life's common plod: still to repair
The body and the thing which perisheth:
The soil, the smutch, the toil and ache and wear,
The grinding enginry of blood and breath,
Pain's random darts, the heartless spade of death;
All is but grief, and heavily we call
On the last terror for the end of all.

Then comes the happy moment: not a stir
In any tree, no portent in the sky:
The morn doth neither hasten nor defer,
The morrow hath no name to call it by,
But life and joy are one,—we know not why,—
As though our very blood long breathless lain
Had tasted of the breath of God again.

And having tasted it I speak of it,
And praise him thinking how I trembled then
When his touch strengthened me, as now I sit
In wonder, reaching out beyond my ken,
Reaching to turn the day back, and my pen
Urging to tell a tale which told would seem
The witless phantasy of them that dream.

But O most blessèd truth, for truth thou art,
Abide thou with me till my life shall end.
Divinity hath surely touched my heart;
I have possessed more joy than earth can lend:
I may attain what time shall never spend.
Only let not my duller days destroy
The memory of thy witness and my joy.

XIV.

THE full moon from her cloudless skies
Turneth her face, I think, on me;
And from the hour when she doth rise
Till when she sets, none else will see.

One only other ray she hath,
That makes an angle close with mine,
And glancing down its happy path
Upon another spot doth shine.

But that ray too is sent to me,
For where it lights there dwells my heart:
And if I were where I would be,
Both rays would shine, love, where thou art.

XV.

AWAKE, my heart, to be loved, awake, awake!
The darkness silvers away, the morn doth break,
It leaps in the sky: unrisen lustres slake
The o'ertaken moon. Awake, O heart, awake!

She too that loveth awaketh and hopes for thee:
Her eyes already have sped the shades that flee,
Already they watch the path thy feet shall take:
Awake, O heart, to be loved, awake, awake!

And if thou tarry from her,—if this could be,—
She cometh herself, O heart, to be loved, to thee;
For thee would unashamèd herself forsake:
Awake to be loved, my heart, awake, awake!

Awake, the land is scattered with light, and see,
Uncanopied sleep is flying from field and tree:
And blossoming boughs of April in laughter shake;
Awake, O heart, to be loved, awake awake!

Lo all things wake and tarry and look for thee:
She looketh and saith, 'O sun now bring him to me.
Come more adored, O adored, for his coming's sake,
And awake my heart to be loved: awake, awake!'

XVI.

SONG.

I LOVE my lady's eyes
Above the beauties rare
She most is wont to prize,
Above her sunny hair,
And all that face to face
Her glass repeats of grace.

For those are still the same
To her and all that see:
But oh! her eyes will flame
When they do look on me:
And so above the rest
I love her eyes the best.

Now say [*Say, O say! saith the music*]
    Who likes my song?—
I knew you by your eyes,
That rest on nothing long,
And have forgot surprise;
And stray [*Stray, O stray! saith the music*]
    as mine will stray,
The while my love 's away.

XVII.

SINCE thou, O fondest and truest,
Hast loved me best and longest,

And now with trust the strongest
The joy of my heart renewest;

Since thou art dearer and dearer
While other hearts grow colder,
And ever, as love is older,
More lovingly drawest nearer:

Since now I see in the measure
Of all my giving and taking,
Thou wert my hand in the making,
The sense and soul of my pleasure;

The good I have ne'er repaid thee
In heaven I pray be recorded,
And all thy love rewarded
By God, thy master that made thee.

XVIII.

THE evening darkens over.
After a day so bright
The windcapt waves discover
That wild will be the night.
There's sound of distant thunder.

The latest sea-birds hover
Along the cliff's sheer height;
As in the memory wander
Last flutterings of delight,
White wings lost on the white.

There's not a ship in sight;
And as the sun goes under
Thick clouds conspire to cover
The moon that should rise yonder.
Thou art alone, fond lover.

XIX.

O YOUTH whose hope is high,
Who dost to Truth aspire,
Whether thou live or die,
O look not back nor tire.

Thou that art bold to fly
Through tempest, flood and fire,
Nor dost not shrink to try
Thy heart in torments dire:

If thou canst Death defy,
If thy Faith is entire,
Press onward, for thine eye
Shall see thy heart's desire.

Beauty and love are nigh,
And with their deathless quire
Soon shall thine eager cry
Be numbered and expire.

BOOK IV.

F

I.

I LOVE all beauteous things,
　　I seek and adore them ;
God hath no better praise,
And man in his hasty days
　　Is honoured for them.

I too will something make
　　And joy in the making ;
Altho' to-morrow it seem
Like the empty words of a dream
　　Remembered on waking.

II.

MY spirit sang all day
　　O my joy.
Nothing my tongue could say,
　　Only My joy !

My heart an echo caught—
　　O my joy—
And spake, Tell me thy thought,
　　Hide not thy joy.

My eyes gan peer around,—
　　O my joy—
What beauty hast thou found ?
　　Shew us thy joy.

F 2

My jealous ears grew whist;—
  O my joy—
Music from heaven is 't,
  Sent for our joy?

She also came and heard;
  O my joy,
What, said she, is this word?
  What is thy joy?

And I replied, O see,
  O my joy,
'Tis thee, I cried, 'tis thee:
  Thou art my joy.

III.

THE upper skies are palest blue
Mottled with pearl and fretted snow:
With tattered fleece of inky hue
Close overhead the stormclouds go.

Their shadows fly along the hill
And o'er the crest mount one by one:
The whitened planking of the mill
Is now in shade and now in sun.

IV.

THE clouds have left the sky,
The wind hath left the sea,
The half-moon up on high
Shrinketh her face of dree.

She lightens on the comb
Of leaden waves, that roar
And thrust their hurried foam
Up on the dusky shore.

Behind the western bars
The shrouded day retreats,
And unperceived the stars
Steal to their sovran seats.

And whiter grows the foam,
The small moon lightens more;
And as I turn me home,
My shadow walks before.

V.

LAST WEEK OF FEBRUARY, 1890.

HARK to the merry birds, hark how they sing!
  Although 'tis not yet spring
    And keen the air;
Hale Winter, half resigning ere he go,
  Doth to his heiress shew
    His kingdom fair.

In patient russet is his forest spread,
  All bright with bramble red,
    With beechen moss
And holly sheen: the oak silver and stark
  Sunneth his aged bark
    And wrinkled boss.

But neath the ruin of the withered brake
  Primroses now awake
    From nursing shades:
The crumpled carpet of the dry leaves brown
  Avails not to keep down
    The hyacinth blades.

The hazel hath put forth his tassels ruffed;
  The willow's flossy tuft
    Hath slipped him free:

The rose amid her ransacked orange hips
    Braggeth the tender tips
      Of bowers to be.

A black rook stirs the branches here and there,
    Foraging to repair
      His broken home :
And hark, on the ash boughs! Never thrush did sing
    Louder in praise of spring,
      When spring is come.

VI.

APRIL, 1885.

WANTON with long delay the gay spring leaping
    cometh ;
The blackthorn starreth now his bough on the eve
    of May :
All day in the sweet box-tree the bee for pleasure
    hummeth :
The cuckoo sends afloat his note on the air all day.

Now dewy nights again and rain in gentle shower
At root of tree and flower have quenched the winter's
    drouth.
On high the hot sun smiles, and banks of cloud uptower
In bulging heads that crowd for miles the dazzlin
    south.

VII.

GÁY Róbin is seen no more :
    He is gone with the snow,
      For winter is o'er
      And Robin will go.
In need he was fed, and now he is fled

Away to his secret nest.
No more will he stand
Begging for crumbs,
No longer he comes
Beseeching our hand
And showing his breast
At window and door ;
Gay Robin is seen no more.

Blithe Robin is heard no more:
He gave us his song
When summer was o'er
And winter was long :
He sang for his bread and now he is fled
Away to his secret nest.
And there in the green
Early and late
Alone to his mate
He pipeth unseen
And swelleth his breast.
For us it is o'er,
Blithe Robin is heard no more.

VIII.

SPRING goeth all in white,
Crowned with milk-white may :
In fleecy flocks of light
O'er heaven the white clouds stray :

    White butterflies in the air ;
White daisies prank the ground :
The cherry and hoary pear
Scatter their snow around.

✓

IX.

My eyes for beauty pine,
My soul for Goddës grace:
No other care nor hope is mine,
To heaven I turn my face.

One splendour thence is shed
From all the stars above:
'Tis namèd when God's name is said,
'Tis Love, 'tis heavenly Love.

And every gentle heart,
That burns with true desire,
Is lit from eyes that mirror part
Of that celestial fire.

X.

O Love, my muse, how was't for me
Among the best to dare,
In thy high courts that bowed the knee
With sacrifice and prayer?
Their mighty offerings at thy shrine
Shamed me, who nothing bore:
Their suits were mockeries of mine,
I sued for so much more.
Full many I met that crowned with bay
In triumph home returned,
And many a master on the way
Proud of the prize I scorned.
I wished no garland on my head
Nor treasure in my hand;
My gift the longing that me led,
My prayer thy high command,

My love, my muse; and when I spake
    Thou mad'st me thine that day,
And more than hundred hearts could take
    Gav'st me to bear away.

XI.

LOVE on my heart from heaven fell,
Soft as the dew on flowers of spring,
Sweet as the hidden drops that swell
Their honey-throated chalicing.

Now never from him do I part,
Hosanna evermore I cry:
I taste his savour in my heart,
And bid all praise him as do I.

Without him noughtsoever is,
Nor was afore, nor e'er shall be:
Nor any other joy than his
Wish I for mine to comfort me.

XII.

THE hill pines were sighing,
O'ercast and chill was the day:
A mist in the valley lying
Blotted the pleasant May.

But deep in the glen's bosom
Summer slept in the fire
Of the odorous gorse-blossom
And the hot scent of the brier.

A ribald cuckoo clamoured,
And out of the copse the stroke
Of the iron axe that hammered
The iron heart of the oak.

Anon a sound appalling,
As a hundred years of pride
Crashed, in the silence falling:
And the shadowy pine-trees sighed.

XIII.

THE WINDMILL.

THE green corn waving in the dale,
The ripe grass waving on the hill:
I lean across the paddock pale
And gaze upon the giddy mill.

Its hurtling sails a mighty sweep
Cut thro' the air: with rushing sound
Each strikes in fury down the steep,
Rattles, and whirls in chase around.

Beside his sacks the miller stands
On high within the open door:
A book and pencil in his hands,
His grist and meal he reckoneth o'er.

His tireless merry slave the wind
Is busy with his work to-day:
From whencesoe'er he comes to grind;
He hath a will and knows the way.

He gives the creaking sails a spin,
The circling millstones faster flee,
The shuddering timbers groan within,
And down the shoots the meal runs free.

The miller giveth him no thanks,
And doth not much his work o'erlook:
He stands beside the sacks, and ranks
The figures in his dusty book.

XIV.

When June is come, then all the day
I'll sit with my love in the scented hay:
And watch the sunshot palaces high,
That the white clouds build in the breezy sky.

She singeth, and I do make her a song,
And read sweet poems the whole day long:
Unseen as we lie in our haybuilt home.
O life is delight when June is come.

XV.

The pinks along my garden walks
Have all shot forth their summer stalks,
Thronging their buds 'mong tulips hot,
   . And blue forget-me-not.

Their dazzling snows forth-bursting soon
Will lade the idle breath of June :
And waken thro' the fragrant night
    To steal the pale moonlight.

The nightingale at end of May
Lingers each year for their display ;
Till when he sees their blossoms blown,
    He knows the spring is flown.

June's birth they greet, and when their bloom
Dislustres, withering on his tomb,
Then summer hath a shortening day ;
    And steps slow to decay.

XVI.

FIRE of heaven, whose starry arrow
Pierces the veil of timeless night:
Molten spheres, whose tempests narrow
Their floods to a beam of gentle light:
To charm with a moon-ray quenched from fire
The land of delight, the land of desire!

Smile of love, a flower planted,
Sprung in the garden of joy that art:
Eyes that shine witha glow enchanted,
Whose spreading fires encircle my heart,
And warm with a noon-ray drenched in fire
My land of delight, my land of desire!

XVII.

THE idle life I lead
Is like a pleasant sleep,
Wherein I rest and heed
The dreams that by me sweep.

And still of all my dreams
In turn so swiftly past,
Each in its fancy seems
A nobler than the last.

And every eve I say,
Noting my step in bliss,
That I have known no day
In all my life like this.

XVIII.

ANGEL spirits of sleep,
White-robed, with silver hair,
In your meadows fair,
Where the willows weep,
And the sad moonbeam
On the gliding stream
Writes her scattered dream:

  Angel spirits of sleep,
Dancing to the weir
In the hollow roar
Of its waters deep;
Know ye how men say
That ye haunt no more
Isle and grassy shore
With your moonlit play;
That ye dance not here,
White-robed spirits of sleep,
All the summer night
Threading dances light?

XIX.

ANNIVERSARY

WHAT is sweeter than new-mown hay,
Fresher than winds o'er sea that blow,
Innocent above children's play,
Fairer and purer than winter snow,
Frolic as are the morns of May?
  —If it should be what best Iknow!

What is richer than thoughts that stray
From reading of poems that smoothly flow?
What is solemn like the delay

Of concords linked in a music slow
Dying thro' vaulted aisles away?
  —If it should be what best I know!

What gives faith to me when I pray,
Setteth my heart with joy aglow,
Filleth my song with fancies gay,
Maketh the heaven to which I go,
The gladness of earth that lasteth for aye?
  —If it should be what best I know!

But tell me thou—'twas on this day
That first we loved five years ago—
If 'tis a thing that I can say,
  Though it must be what best we know.

XX.

THE summer trees are tempest-torn,
The hills are wrapped in a mantle wide
Of folding rain by the mad wind borne
  Across the country side.

His scourge of fury is lashing down
The delicate-rankèd golden corn,
That never more shall rear its crown
  And curtsey to the morn.

There shews no care in heaven to save
Man's pitiful patience, or provide
A season for the season's slave,
  Whose trust hath toiled and died.

So my proud spirit in me is sad,
A wreck of fairer fields to mourn,
The ruin of golden hopes she had,
  My delicate-rankèd corn.

XXI.

THE birds that sing on autumn eves
Among the golden-tinted leaves,
Are but the few that true remain
Of budding May's rejoicing train.

Like autumn flowers that brave the frost,
And make their show when hope is lost,
These 'mong the fruits and mellow scent
Mourn not the high-sunned summer spent.

Their notes thro' all the jocund spring
Were mixed in merry musicking:
They sang for love the whole day long,
But now their love is all for song.

Now each hath perfected his lay
To praise the year that hastes away:
They sit on boughs apart, and vie
In single songs and rich reply:

And oft as in the copse I hear
These anthems of the dying year,
The passions, once her peace that stole,
With flattering love my heart console.

XXII.

WHEN my love was away,
Full three days were not sped,
I caught my fancy astray
Thinking if she were dead,

And I alone, alone:
It seemed in my misery
In all the world was none
Ever so lone as I.

I wept; but it did not shame
Nor comfort my heart: away
I rode as I might, and came
To my love at close of day.

The sight of her stilled my fears,
My fairest-hearted love:
And yet in her eyes were tears:
Which when I questioned of,

O now thou art come, she cried,
'Tis fled: but I thought to-day
I never could here abide,
If thou wert longer away.

XXIII.

THE storm is over, the land hushes to rest:
The tyrannous wind, its strength fordone,
Is fallen back in the west
To couch with the sinking sun.
The last clouds fare
With fainting speed, and their thin streamers fly
In melting drifts of the sky.
Already the birds in the air
Appear again; the rooks return to their haunt,
And one by one,
Proclaiming aloud their care,
Renew their peaceful chant.

Torn and shattered trees their branches again reset,
They trim afresh the fair
Few green and golden leaves withheld from the storm,
And awhile will be handsome yet.
To-morrow's sun shall caress
Their remnant of loveliness:

In quiet days for a time
Sad Autumn lingering warm
Shall humour their faded prime.

But ah! the leaves of summer that lie on the ground!
What havoc! The laughing timbrels of June,
That curtained the birds' cradles, and screened their
    song,
That sheltered the cooing doves at noon,
Of airy fans the delicate throng,—
Torn and scattered around:
Far out afield they lie,
In the watery furrows die,
In grassy pools of the flood they sink and drown,
Green-golden, orange, vermilion, golden and brown,
The high year's flaunting crown
Shattered and trampled down.

The day is done: the tired land looks for night:
She prays to the night to keep
In peace her nerves of delight:
While silver mist upstealeth silently,
And the broad cloud-driving moon in the clear sky
Lifts o'er the firs her shining shield,
And in her tranquil light
Sleep falls on forest and field.
Sée! sléep hath fallen: the trees are asleep:
The night is come. The land is wrapt in sleep.

XXIV.

YE thrilled me once, ye mournful strains,
  Ye anthems of plaintive woe,
My spirit was sad when I was young;
  Ah sorrowful long-ago!

G

But since I have found the beauty of joy,
  I have done with proud dismay:
For howsoe'er man hug his care
  The best of his art is gay.

And yet if voices of fancy's choir
  Again in mine ear awake
Your old lament, 'tis dear to me still,
  Nor all for memory's sake:
'Tis like the dirge of sorrow dead,
  Whose tears are wiped away;
Or drops of the shower, when rain is o'er,
  That jewel the brightened day.

XXV.

Say who is this with silvered hair,
  So pale and worn and thin,
Who passeth here, and passeth there,
  And looketh out and in?

That useth not our garb nor tongue,
  And knoweth things untold:
Who teacheth pleasure to the young,
  And wisdom to the old?

No toil he maketh his by day,
  No home his own by night;
But wheresoe'er he take his way,
  He killeth our delight.

Since he is come there's nothing wise
  Nor fair in man or child,
Unless his deep divining eyes
  Have looked on it and smiled.

Whence came he hither all alone
  Among our folk to spy?
There 's nought that we can call our own,
  Till he shall hap to die.

And I would dig his grave full deep
  Beneath the churchyard yew,
Lest thence his wizard eyes might peep
  To mark the things we do.

XXVI.

CROWN Winter with green,
And give him good drink
To physic his spleen
Or ever he think.

His mouth to the bowl,
His feet to the fire ;
And let him, good soul,
No comfort desire.

So merry he be,
I bid him abide :
And merry be we
This good Yuletide.

XXVII.

THE snow lies sprinkled on the beach,
And whitens all the marshy lea :
The sad gulls wail adown the gale,
The day is dark and black the sea.
  Shorn of their crests the blighted waves
With driven foam the offing fleck :
The ebb is low and barely laves
The red rust of the giant wreck.

On such a stony, breaking beach
My childhood chanced and chose to be:
'Twas here I played, and musing made
My friend the melancholy sea.
　He from his dim enchanted caves
With shuddering roar and onrush wild
Fell down in sacrificial waves
At feet of his exulting child.

Unto a spirit too light for fear
His wrath was mirth, his wail was glee:—
My heart is now too fixed to bow
Tho' all his tempests howl at me:
　For to the gain life's summer saves,
My solemn joy's increasing store,
The tossing of his mournful waves
Makes sweetest music evermore.

XXVIII.

My spirit kisseth thine,
My spirit embraceth thee:
I feel thy being twine
Her graces over me,

　In the life-kindling fold
Of God's breath; where on high,
In furthest space untold
Like a lost world I lie:

　And o'er my dreaming plains
Lightens, most pale and fair,
A moon that never wanes;
Or more, if I compare,

Like what the shepherd sees
On late mid-winter dawns,
When thro' the branchèd trees,
O'er the white-frosted lawns,

The huge unclouded sun,
Surprising the world whist,
Is all uprisen thereon,
Golden with melting mist.

XXIX.

ARIEL, O,—my angel, my own,—
Whither away then art thou flown
    Beyond my spirit's dominion?
That makest my heart run over with rhyme,
Renewing at will my youth for a time,
    My servant, my pretty minion.

Now indeed I have cause to mourn,
Now thou returnest scorn for scorn:
    Leave me not to my folly:
For when thou art with me is none so gay
As I, and none when thou'rt away
    Was ever so melancholy.

XXX.

LAUS DEO.

LET praise devote thy work, and skill employ
Thy whole mind, and thy heart be lost in joy.
Well-doing bringeth pride, this constant thought
Humility, that thy best done is nought.
Man doeth nothing well, be it great or small,
Save to praise God; but that hath savèd all:
For God requires no more than thou hast done,
And takes thy work to bless it for his own.

NOTE.

The poems contained in Book I are my final selection from a volume published in 1873. Those of Book II are from a pamphlet published in 1879. Some of all these are in places corrected. Book III is made up of poems from a pamphlet published in 1880; to which are added others of about the same date. Some of these have already appeared in a volume printed for me by my friend the Rev. C. H. Daniel, in 1884. No. 6 was written to a tune by Dr. Howard. No. 19 is a pretty close translation of a poem by Théophile Gautier, which is itself a translation from the English by Thomas Moore in The Epicurean. All the poems in Book IV are now printed for the first time. No. 9 is a translation from a madrigal by Michael Angelo, (No. VIII in Guasti). It is from my Comedy 'The Humours of the Court,' in which also No. 16 occurs. No. 11 is from a Sicilian nona rima stanza, the first poem in Trucchi's Poesie Italiane inedite.

R. B.

YATTENDON, 1890.

INDEX OF FIRST LINES.

www.ingramcontent.com/pod-product-compliance
Lightning Source LLC
Chambersburg PA
CBHW020035030726
47499CB00007B/2433